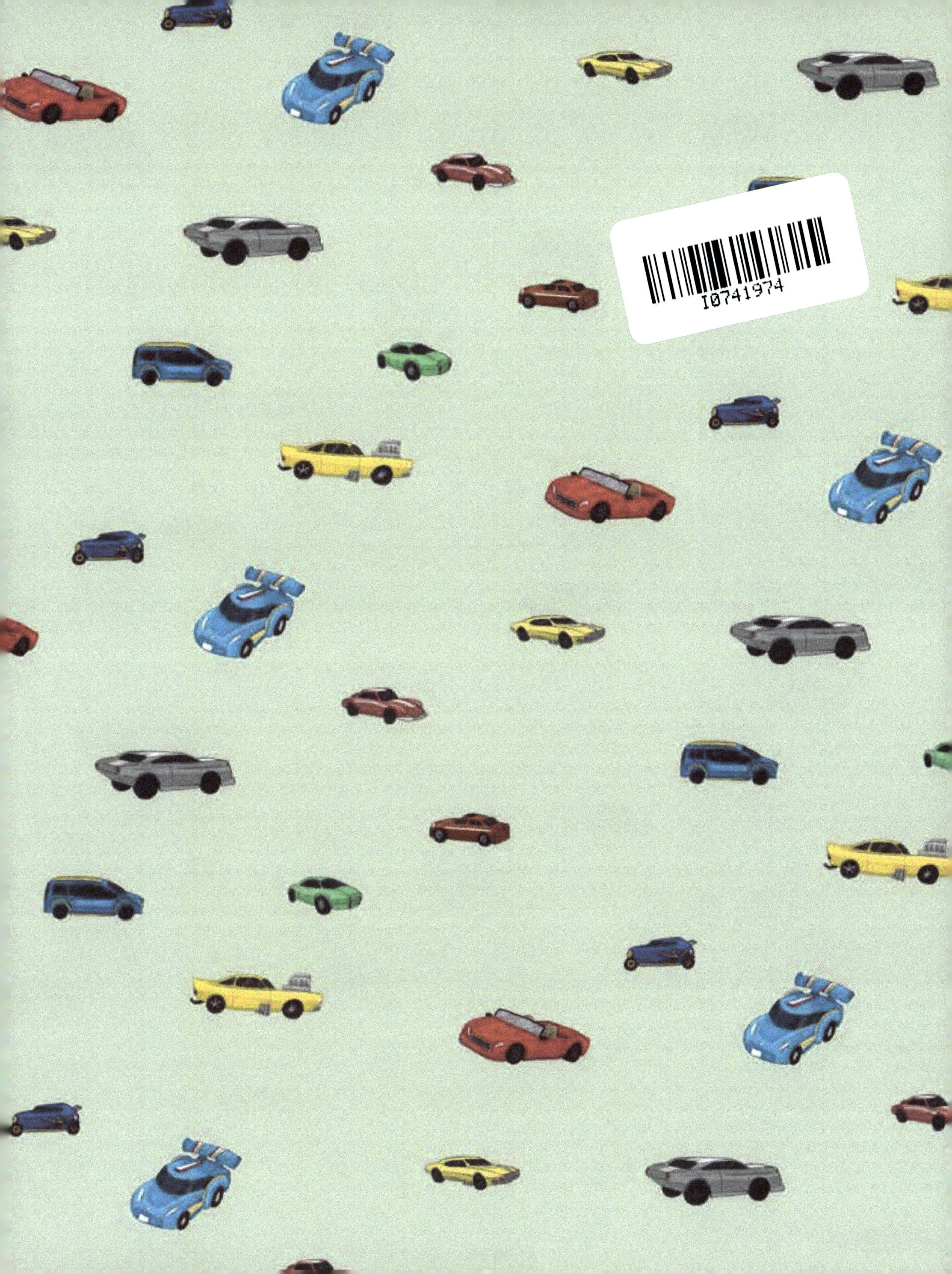

I0741974

To my family, thank you for all your love and support.

Davahr, thank you for always teaching me about the world through your eyes.

Damian Jr., I admire how you take on the world. No challenge is too great for you.

Dahkari, you are serving your purpose and it becomes clearer with each passing day.

Damian, thank you for being who you are.

www.mascotbooks.com

DIFFERENT BUT SPECIAL

For more information, please contact:
Mascot Kids, an imprint of Amplify Publishing Group
620 Herndon Parkway #320
Herndon, VA 20170
info@mascotbooks.com

CPSIA Code: PRKF0922A
Library of Congress Control Number: 2022945624

Printed in China

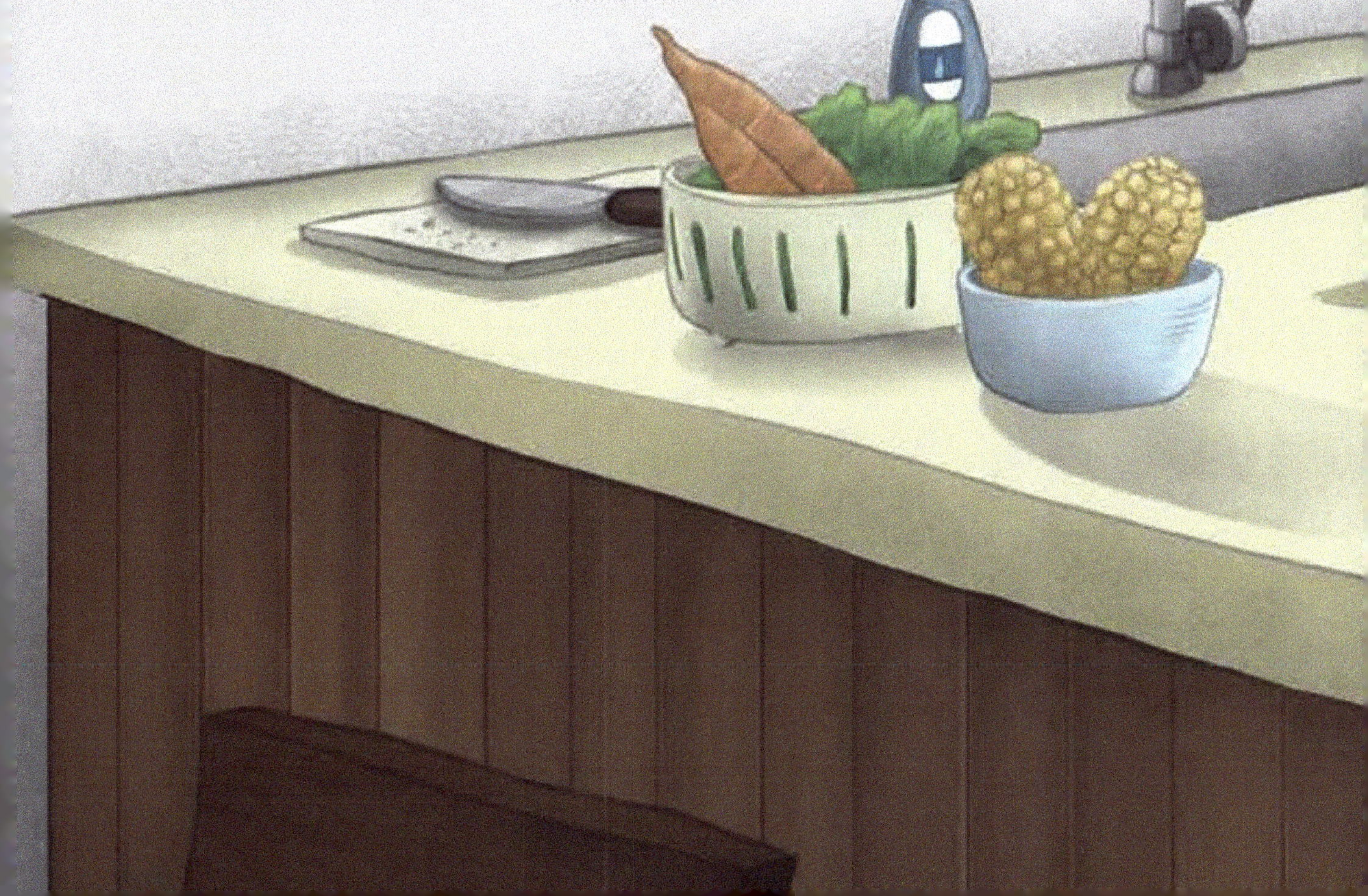

DIFFERENT
BUT
SPECIAL
SUSAN VANRIEL-SMITH
Illustrated by Agus Prajogo and Yohanes Bastian

Nicholas is an eight-year-old boy who loves playing with toy cars. He has hundreds of toy cars. But, unlike other children, he likes to play with them by himself and have them in specific places in his room. "Vroom! Vroom! Clank! Clank!" These are the sounds that usually come from Nicholas's room.

Nicholas has autism and acts younger than his age. He mostly uses gestures, or pictures and words on his special device, to talk to others. Nicholas can say words but has to be encouraged by his family to do so. He often repeats their words, although he may not understand them. Lots of children have autism, and their loved ones learn their special languages too!

But a day in Nicholas's life can be quite an adventure. Like today! It is Saturday and Mom is preparing Nicholas for church tomorrow. Planning and preparation make events easier for Nicholas.

Thump! Thump! Thump! Banging noises are coming through Michael's bedroom wall.

"Knock it off!" shouts Michael. "Mom! Nicholas is jumping again, and I can't hear the TV."

Mom walks into Nicholas's room. "Nicholas, please sit, no jumping.
It's not safe, ok?"

But Nicholas won't listen. One minute later, he jumps again. This time
Mom says it louder. "No, Nicki! No jumping, you'll get hurt. It is not safe."

Nicholas does not like it when Mommy uses her loud voice, so he stops jumping, calms down, and starts playing on his tablet. He likes to play games like Candy Crush and Bowling.

On the way back downstairs, Mom stops at Michael's room to check on him.

Michael mumbles, "I wish my little brother wasn't so different and was more like Tommy's little brother." Tommy has been Michael's best friend since kindergarten.

Mom hugs Michael. She holds his face in her hands and says, "I love you both with all my heart. There will be some difficult times, but please remember: Nicholas is different, but he is very special to our family and we love him just the way he is. Michael, do you promise to always have your brother's back?" asks Mom gently.

"I promise, Mom," says Michael. Mom kisses him and goes back downstairs.

On her way down, she pauses on the stairs when she hears footsteps. It is Michael. He is going to Nicholas's room.

Then she hears, "I love you little bro, and you're special to me." Michael then says, "Tomorrow is Sunday, Nicholas, and we are going to church." Life is much easier for Nicholas if he knows what is next. Repetition is important for him.

Mom goes down the stairs after hearing laughter and playing. She is so happy that they get along and that Michael is helping his brother.

Inside Nicholas's room, Michael gets up from the floor and says, "Come on Nicholas, let's find your outfit for church." Nicholas jumps up, very excited. He jumps a few times before heading to the closet.

Michael lays three different pants on the bed. Nicholas has to choose from brown, blue, or black. He stares at them while Michael patiently waits. Nicholas picks the blue pants. Before Michael can say, "Good job Nikki," Nicholas is already bringing a shirt from the closet. Michael doesn't think it's the best choice, but he does not change the shirt.

They both sit down on the floor to decide which shoes Nicholas
should wear. Michael picks a black pair of shoes, but Nicholas
says, "No," pushing it away and grabbing the blue ones instead.
Nicholas gets up and goes back to playing with his toys.

Later, Michael comes downstairs to see if Mom needs help with dinner. He hugs her and says, "I love having a special little brother, he can be very fun. I wish he would talk to me though."

"I believe he will one day, Michael."

While helping his mom with dinner, Michael tells her that he prepared Nicholas for church.

"I showed him his clothes and church shoes, and then made sure I put them back in the right places. I didn't want him to cry and throw things. I know everything has to be in the right place or Nicholas will have a meltdown."

Mom looks at him, hugs him, and says, "Michael, what would I do without you?" Michael feels so happy that he helped.

Later, Dad comes home and, as usual, Nicholas runs down the stairs to meet him. Nicholas and Dad always do fun things together. Sometimes Dad holds his hands and Nicholas jumps as high as possible in the kitchen. Nicholas also likes to bring Dad to the living room so they can play pillow fight or the tickle game. The tickle game is Dad tickling Nicholas and saying, "C'mere bwoy," with a Jamaican accent. Nicholas's laughter makes everyone else laugh. They all love to watch him laugh and play.

At dinner, everyone tries to not have any gadgets and engage with each other. This is hard for Nicholas, as he needs something to do while he eats. Sometimes he has the iPad and puts on a video or plays a game. Other times he has a toy that plays music.

While Nikki is eating, everything has its place. The place mat must be facing the right direction. The bowl must be in the right spot. The cup must be to his right and in front of the bowl. The spoon must be toward the right-hand side of the bowl. And in front of Nikki's place mat, there is always a toy ambulance and a white car. Even those must be parked in their exact spots before he begins to eat.

After dinner, Nikki goes to his room. He prefers to be alone most of the time, and lies under his blanket with the iPad while watching videos or playing educational games. After an hour or two, it is bath time. Nicholas loves bath time because he loves water. He loves water so much that he flushes the toilet just to see the water spin.

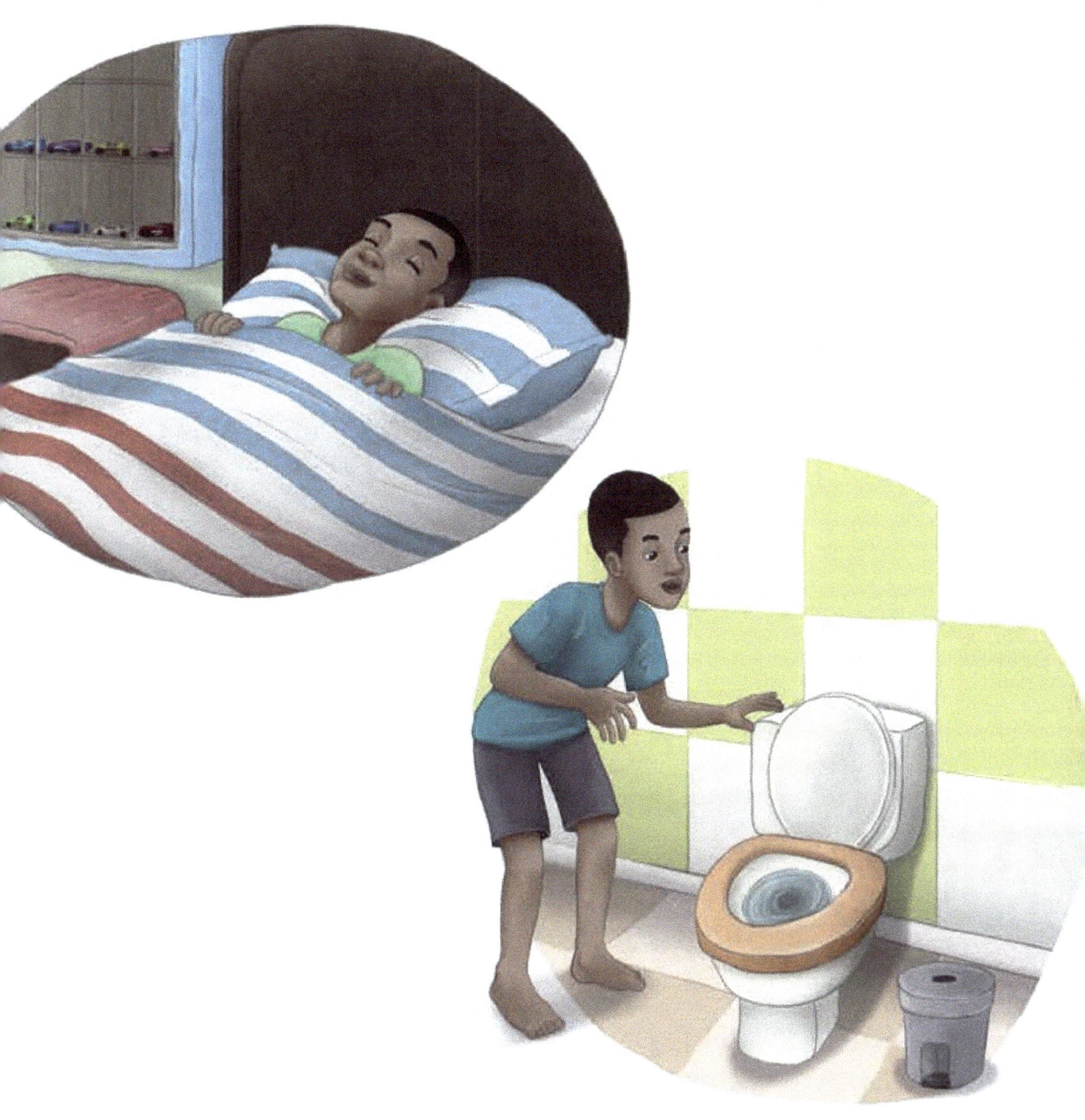

After Nicholas has his bath and brushes his teeth, he lies down and relaxes. After relaxing for a while, he is filled with energy and gets up to run down the hallway. At midnight, when Mom hears Nicholas, she says, "Nicholas, it's sleeping time, close your eyes . . ."

He quiets down, but not for long. Then he is back to sliding down the hall. Finally, Dad goes into his room and lies down with him. Nicholas always falls asleep easier when Dad is with him.

Michael is up bright and early. He wants to eat, be ready for church on time, and help Nicholas.

Mom waits to get Nicholas dressed last because he can get upset if he has to wait for a long time to leave the house. Nicholas is in a good mood today, until Mom would not allow him to wear a tie. He likes wearing ties to church, but this shirt didn't need one. Nicholas starts screaming and knocking things off the dresser. Eventually, Mom has to give him the tie, whether it goes with his shirt or not. This makes him smile, and he is happy again.

Nicholas's favorite part about church is snack time. His favorite snacks are packed because it's lunch time for him when they get to church. He eats with Michael in the break room. They finish eating and come back to the congregation. Nikki is calm, listens to the music, and even claps and rocks back and forth to the beat of the music. He is tired and dozes off toward the end of the service.

Michael is so proud of Nicholas's behavior that he hugs him outside and says,

"Nicholas, I love you so much, you are such an awesome lil' bro."

Dad and Mom join in on the hug too.

They all celebrate what may seem like something small to others, but in fact is a huge victory for their family.

All together they say, "Nicholas you may be different, but—" Before they can finish the sentence, Nicholas claps his hands and then, in a loud and clear voice, yells, "Special!"

What more could they ask for on this Sunday? They hug some more and chuckle before heading home.

AbOuT tHe AuThOr

Susan Vanriel-Smith is a registered polysomnographer. She has a bachelor's in biology from Eastern Connecticut State University, and a master's in biology from the University of Saint Joseph. Susan loves to read, and her hobbies include anything in which she can be creative. She is originally from the island of Jamaica, but now lives in Connecticut with her husband and three boys. Her first two sons were diagnosed on the autism spectrum when they were much younger, and they inspired the creation of this book. Each day can be challenging, but as a family they work together to get through it. Susan hopes that this book can be of help to other families that face similar situations. Susan also has an online store that is primarily dedicated to bringing awareness to autism and promoting acceptance and inclusion.

giftedoneprinces.com

@giftedoneprinces